leisure & ulture DUNDEE

The Wish Pony

Written by Lisa Thompson

Illustrated by Molly Sage

Better ways to learn

Saddleback Stables: The Wish Pony
ISBN: 978 1 76020 163 0

 Lexile®Measure: 640L
For more information visit www.lexile.com
Lexile © 2013 MetaMetrics, Inc.

Text copyright © 2018 Lisa Thompson
Written by Lisa Thompson
Illustrations copyright © 2018 Blake Publishing
Illustrated by Molly Sage

Published by Blake Education Pty Ltd
ABN 50 074 266 023
108 Main Road
Clayton South VIC 3169
info@blake.com.au
www.blake.com.au

Publisher: Katy Pike
Series editor: Mark Stafford
Page layout: Modern Art Production Group
Printer: 1010 Printing Asia Limited

CONTENTS

Jordy

Chief

Sophie

Biscu

Hannah

Jin Jin

Bella

Gypsy Rose

Alexa

Billy Blaze

4

CHAPTER ONE

Hannah's Wish Pony

Hannah's greatest wish was for a pony. Her wish pony had a shiny coat, a thick flowing mane and a beautiful long tail that floated like a ribbon. Hannah's wish pony was clever, kind and trusting. Together they would be a **perfect team**.

Hannah sometimes visited Aunt Ruby's farm to ride Henry, her aunt's Shetland pony. Henry was kind and trusting ... but he was also old and stubborn. When he was in the paddock by himself, he was full of **energy**. But when Hannah was in the saddle, Henry just plodded along. He was definitely not Hannah's **wish pony**.

One afternoon Hannah's mum had big news: they were moving! Their new home was near Saddleback Stables Riding School.

"I'm sure they'll have a great pony for you to ride," said Mum. "Maybe one like your wish pony."

One morning, a few weeks after moving to her new home, Hannah's mum and dad burst into her room.

"Happy birthday!" they cried.

Hannah struggled to open her eyes. She'd just had the most beautiful dream about riding her wish pony.

"Come on," teased Mum. "Let's get this birthday started."

"How about the big present first," said Dad. He handed Hannah a card.

Hannah opened it. She was expecting
to see a photo of her beautiful wish
pony inside, or maybe simply its name
written in gold letters. Instead, it was
a gift voucher for riding lessons at
Saddleback Stables.

"We signed you up for a whole year!"
said Mum.

"Miss Jill, who owns the stables, said you're welcome to pop over any time you like," said Dad. "She's always looking for kids keen to care for the school ponies once lessons are over."

School ponies? Hannah didn't want to cry, so she bit her bottom lip.

"What's the matter?" asked Mum. "We thought this would be a perfect present."

Hannah hesitated. "It's just I was expecting … I was hoping …" She took a deep breath then **blurted**, "I was hoping for a pony. My wish pony."

"Oh, Hannah," said Mum gently. "A pony is not something we can afford right now."

Hannah nodded because, deep down inside, she understood this all along.

"When I win the **lottery**," said Dad and winked, "I promise you'll get your pony and your mother and I will get that golfing holiday we've always dreamed about."

"**Golf?** I don't dream about golf," said Hannah's mum with a laugh.

Hannah's dad pretended to be shocked and then smiled at Hannah. "Come on, my new ten-year-old," he said. "There's a small **mountain** of presents waiting for you on the dining table. There may be something to wear on those feet of yours when you head over to Saddleback Stables."

"Your first riding lesson is this morning!" said Mum, sounding **extra cheery**. "I'll take you over after breakfast."

9

CHAPTER TWO

Saddleback Stables

Hannah and her mum stood outside a small shed at Saddleback Stables. The office door was locked.

"**Over here**!" came a call from behind them.

A man with a mop of grey hair and a **bushy beard** waved from near the stables. He wore blue overalls, a checked shirt and gumboots. Hannah and her mum walked over to meet him.

"Morning, I'm Bill the stables manager," he said and nodded to Hannah. "You're starting lessons today, right? Miss Jill filled me in."

Hannah looked down at her **brand new** riding boots. She suddenly felt a little shy. They were very **shiny** next to Bill's well-worn boots.

"Are we early?" asked Hannah's mum. "There don't seem to be any other riders here."

"Someone's over in the tack room," said Bill. "Come on, Hannah, I'll take you over to meet her."

Hannah waved goodbye to her mum and followed Bill. She immediately stepped in a puddle, **splashing** her riding boots with mud. Hannah smiled. She didn't want shiny boots when she met the other riders. They might think she'd never been near a pony before!

"Morning!" called Bill into a small room packed with leads, bridles, ropes, helmets, rugs and saddles. A girl about Hannah's age was standing next to a pile of saddle blankets. She was shorter than Hannah and had thick, black hair.

"Sophie Chen, this is Hannah Harrison," said Bill. "She's joining your class today."

"Hi," said Sophie with a **toothy grin**.

"Can you help Hannah get her pony ready? Miss Jill said she'll be riding Jin Jin."

"**Jin Jin**?" Sophie gave Bill a funny look.

"That's what I said," replied Bill. "Now, I'm off to check how Jordy is going with Chief."

"Jordy is in our class too," explained Sophie after Bill left. "He's really good. Chief is one of the stable ponies. He can be tricky to catch, but Jordy has a talent for handling stubborn ponies."

Hannah liked Sophie immediately. She was **So friendly**!

"Jin Jin's in the same paddock as Biscuit, the pony I ride," continued Sophie. "Have you ridden much?"

"A little," said Hannah.

Sophie passed Hannah a helmet, bridle, saddle rug and saddle, and grabbed a set for herself. "Follow me," she said.

After they left the tack room, the girls passed a pony standing quietly in a holding paddock. It was **Silvery-pink** with a golden mane and tail.

"Beautiful, isn't she?" said Sophie. "That's Gypsy Rose. She's a **Strawberry roan**. The mix of white and chestnut hairs makes her look pinkish. Bella just got her—hey, there's Bella."

A girl with dark, curly hair trotted up on a spotted grey pony.

"Hey Bella, why are you on Reba?"

called Sophie. "Shouldn't you be riding Gypsy Rose?"

"Oh, I'll ride her later. Reba spotted me and got **all excited** and I didn't want to disappoint her." Bella turned to Hannah. "Hi, I'm Bella. Bill told me there was a new rider today. Hannah, isn't it?"

Hannah nodded as she rubbed Reba's soft nose. "Is Reba your pony as well as Gypsy Rose?"

"No, Reba belongs to the stables but she feels like mine. I've been riding her most Saturdays and during the week for two years. I got Gypsy Rose just last week. Do you know what pony you're riding?"

"Jin Jin," answered Sophie.

"**Jin Jin?**" said Bella, raising an eyebrow.

"Um, what's that look mean?" asked Hannah warily.

"Well, Jin Jin's very **fussy** about who rides him," said Bella. "He can be really **cheeky**. But Miss Jill knows what she's doing. She wouldn't give you a pony she didn't think you could handle. She matched me with Reba, and Sophie with Biscuit, and we couldn't be happier."

Sophie agreed. "Biscuit is a mischief-maker but I love him. Look, there he is over in the paddock with Jin Jin. Biscuit's the chestnut Shetland and Jin Jin's ..."

"The **patchy one**?" cried Hannah.

"That's him. The tubby skewbald," said Bella with a giggle. "Be careful when you put the saddle on him. He likes to puff out his tummy. He once played that trick on me. My saddle slid sideways and I fell off as soon as we started walking."

Jin Jin didn't look anything like Hannah's wish pony. He was **patchy** and a little **chubby**. His head was a bit too big and his legs a bit too short, even for a pony.

As Hannah sized up Jin Jin, she spotted another pony much more like her wish pony. He had a glistening brown coat and a thick, dark tail that floated as he walked. He had the most beautiful **black-rimmed** eyes and a white **blaze** on his nose.

A girl in beige jodhpurs, brown riding boots and a dark blue riding hat sat tall in the saddle. Her blonde ponytail fell so perfectly down her back that Hannah touched her own hair. She quickly tucked some untidy strands behind her ear.

"Who is that?" asked Hannah, **mesmerised** as the pony and rider trotted past.

"That's Alexa MacKenzie and Billy Blaze," said Sophie. "Whatever you

do, **don't** go near Billy Blaze without asking Alexa."

Hannah guessed that Sophie and Alexa were not exactly best friends.

"You borrowers will be late for your lesson if you don't hurry," called Alexa, not even turning her head as she rode past.

"**Borrowers**?" whispered Hannah.

Sophie rolled her eyes. "It's what Alexa calls anyone who has lessons but doesn't own their pony—like she does."

"Really?" said Hannah. "She's lucky to have such a beautiful pony."

"That's another thing," said Sophie. "Don't call Billy Blaze a **pony**." She thrust her chin out and pretended to be Alexa. "He is a **bay thoroughbred** more than 14 hands high, so that makes him a **horse**."

Hannah watched Alexa and Billy Blaze disappear into the undercover training area at Saddleback Stables.

"I'm glad she's not in our class," said Bella. "Alexa has private lessons."

"Come on," said Sophie. "We'd better get our ponies ready. We shouldn't keep Miss Jill waiting."

CHAPTER THREE

The Lesson

Hannah, Sophie, Bella and Jordy lined up on their ponies in the outdoor training paddock. Jordy had nodded to Hannah when she arrived. He had **dusty** riding boots and **messy** brown hair poking out from beneath his helmet. He sat confidently on the dark grey Chief.

Miss Jill had a kind smile and a no-nonsense attitude. She checked her students' saddles and bridles. She made Hannah's stirrups a little longer and checked she was holding her reins correctly.

"Relax, Hannah," said Miss Jill. "I know you've ridden before, so you've got the basics already. You and Jin Jin are going to get along just fine. Try not to pull on his mouth too much. Use your legs and weight to tell him what you want. He's a bright little pony."

Jin Jin's ears **twitched**, like he knew someone was talking about him.

"Right," said Miss Jill, "let's start with a walk around the arena. Figure eight, please. Then we'll try some trotting, cantering and turns. Jordy, you lead with Chief, and then Bella go with Reba and Sophie with Biscuit. Hannah, you and Jin Jin follow at the end."

The others began walking but Jin Jin wouldn't **budge**. Hannah gave him a little kick, and then another, to get along. **Nothing**. Then she remembered Aunt Ruby telling her to squeeze her legs as well as kick to get old Henry moving.

This worked and Jin Jin moved to join the others. But he didn't like being last—he wanted to walk beside Biscuit and Sophie.

"Pull him into line, Hannah," instructed Miss Jill.

Hannah sat deep in her saddle and held the reins **taut**. Jin Jin knew what she was asking and dropped back to the end of the line. Hannah noticed Jordy turn around and smile.

Hannah soon discovered that Jin Jin was happy to turn left but didn't like to turn right. Hannah focused and remained calm. Jin Jin began to do what she asked.

"Back into line everyone," said Miss Jill. "Now let's practise our trotting."

She set the riders off one by one around the edge of the arena, coaching them from the centre. "Good work, Jordy, nice pace. Watch your elbows, Bella.

Tuck them in—I won't allow **flying chickens** in my class. Sophie, keep your back straight, head up. Don't look at the ground! Right, Hannah, it's your turn."

Before Hannah was ready, Jin Jin took off in a **bouncy trot**. Hannah bobbed up and down, hardly in control.

"Find the rhythm, Hannah!" called Miss Jill. "Slow him up a little and get in time—up, down, up, down."

Hannah found the rhythm after a few more wobbly bumps. But then Jin Jin broke into a canter! Hannah pulled him back to a rough trot and then slowed him to a walk. She spent most of the rest of the lesson trying to make him trot and then keeping him at it.

Bella was right: Jin Jin was a **challenge**.

"All right everyone, that's enough,"
said Miss Jill. "You did well today. Take
your ponies back to the stables and
wipe them down." Miss Jill nodded to
Hannah. "Good job with Jin Jin."

Hannah smiled but didn't feel like she
had ridden well at all.

The others rode out of the arena, but
Jin Jin decided he'd prefer to stay where
he was.

"Come *on*, Jin Jin," pleaded Hannah, giving him yet another kick along.

"Coming by!" called Alexa, as she and Billy Blaze trotted past.

Jin Jin snorted and pricked his ears. With just the slightest tap from Hannah, he began to trot to the stables. Jin Jin held a steady trot behind Billy Blaze, and Hannah rose in and out of the saddle in **perfect time**.

"Why didn't you behave like this in the lesson?" Hannah whispered to Jin Jin. "Maybe we'll be good for each other after all."

"**Wow!**" said Sophie when she saw Hannah trot up to the stables. "Jin Jin never trots like that for me. He likes your **confidence**." Jin Jin snorted like he understood. "Hey, I'm going to give

Biscuit a wash and braid his mane. You want to do the same?"

"Sure," replied Hannah, "but I've never braided a mane before."

"It's easy," smiled Sophie. "Follow me to my pony pampering salon."

Hannah and Sophie led the ponies around the side of the stables and hosed them down. They rubbed in shampoo, and Sophie showed Hannah how to massage Jin Jin's neck and withers. Jin Jin **Sighed** and **Snuffled**.

The girls hosed off the suds and then dried, brushed and combed the ponies' manes and tails. Jin Jin's coat didn't shine like Billy Blaze's but it was now much softer, and his mane and tail were free of tangles.

Sophie showed Hannah how to braid Jin Jin's mane. "If you can braid your own hair, you can braid a mane." Hannah looked up and noticed Bella **stomping** away from Gypsy Rose in the holding yard. "Why is Bella grumpy?" Hannah thought. "Gypsy Rose is such a beautiful pony."

Just then, Miss Jill came around the side of the stables.

"Look at these beautiful, clean ponies!" she cried. "They're so lucky to have you." Sophie and Hannah smiled proudly. "Hannah, your mum rang to say she'll be here in a minute to pick you up. Please put Jin Jin back in his paddock before you go. **Double-check** the gate before you leave. Jin Jin knows how to open it and let himself out."

Jin Jin snorted, as if to say, "Yes, I'm good at that."

Hannah walked Jin Jin back to his paddock. He nudged her with his nose and sighed.

"I'm going to visit you tomorrow," said Hannah, stroking his neck. "I really liked spending time with you. You know, today is my birthday and my lessons are a birthday present. I guess that makes you my birthday pony." She **tickled** his nose. "I'm glad I met you."

As Hannah drove out of Saddleback Stables with her mum, she saw Bella riding Reba again. Gypsy Rose stood alone in her paddock.

CHAPTER FOUR

A Matter of Trust

As well as Saturday lessons, Hannah spent all her spare time at Saddleback Stables. She looked forward to every minute of it.

One Saturday morning before a lesson, Hannah strolled over to Jin Jin's paddock. The pony immediately trotted towards her with an excited whinny. Hannah's **heart leapt**! Jin Jin was just as happy to see her as she was to see him.

They met at the paddock fence, and Jin Jin sniffed Hannah's pockets. Hannah always arrived with slices of apple. She

stretched her hand out flat and Jin Jin
gobbled up his treat. She rubbed him
between his ears and he **snorted**.

"Ready for a lesson, Jin Jin?"

During Hannah's riding class, Jin Jin
did everything asked of him. Hannah
could feel the trust between them

growing. She was proud when Miss Jill noticed too. After the lesson Jin Jin was still **full of energ**y.

"Why don't you take him for a ride in the top paddock?" suggested Miss Jill. "I'll keep an eye on you while Bill sets up the jumps for the next lesson. Just don't go down the track to the creek. Stay where I can see you."

A trail ran from the top paddock down to Cockatoo Creek. That's where Bella and Sophie took their ponies to cool off on a hot day.

Hannah walked Jin Jin up to the top paddock and then gave him a little kick. They broke into a trot and then into a canter, over to the far fence. Hannah couldn't help but smile. There was something about the feeling of

the wind on her face and the sound
of **hooves striking** the ground that
made her feel so happy, so free. She
imagined Jin Jin felt it too.

As they trotted back across the
paddock, Jin Jin tossed his head and
yanked at the reins. His ears twitched.
He lifted his nose in the air and laid
his ears flat. Something was wrong.

"What is it, Jin Jin?" Hannah asked. A thunderstorm approaching? A snake in the paddock? Jin Jin flattened his ears and pawed at the ground. Hannah looked around but didn't notice anything unusual.

Without warning Jin Jin **daShed** for the start of the trail. He cantered into the bush, refusing Hannah's attempts to stop him. Again and again she tried pulling him up, but as the trail narrowed Jin Jin just ignored her.

They were well down the track when Jin Jin suddenly slowed and neighed. Hannah heard a highly **agitated whinny** from up ahead. And then a voice.

"Come on, Gypsy Rose! *Please!*"

The whinny was replaced by a frightened neigh. Hannah recognised the voice.

"Bella!" she cried. "Bella, it's Hannah! I'm coming."

She tapped Jin Jin to move on and they picked their way down the track to the bank of Cockatoo Creek. Bella sat astride Gypsy Rose on the opposite side of the creek. She was red-eyed from crying.

"Hannah! What am I going to do? I can't get her to cross the creek," said Bella in frustration. "She's afraid. I've walked her up and down, up and down. Reba **never** has a problem with the creek." Bella tried again to get Gypsy Rose to move. "Come on, you **silly pony**!"

Hannah could tell Bella's frustration wasn't helping. Gypsy Rose needed to feel safe and calm before she'd cross.

"If she sees Jin Jin in the water, maybe she'll change her mind," suggested Hannah.

Hannah **nudged** her pony forward. He stepped into the water calmly, slowly making his way to the middle of the creek. Hannah let him drop his head for a noisy drink. Jin Jin made his way closer to Bella and Gypsy Rose and then stopped for another drink.

Gypsy Rose took a few steps into the creek. She stood beside Jin Jin for a moment before deciding she also wanted to drink.

Cockatoo
Creek

39

"**Good girl**, Gypsy Rose," said Bella, "and good on you, Jin Jin! Let her know there's nothing to be afraid of."

Hannah gave Jin Jin a proud pat and turned him around. They slowly walked out of the creek. Gypsy Rose and Bella followed and began making their way back up the track.

"Thank goodness you two showed up," said Bella. "Who knows how long we would have been stuck there. That wouldn't have happened with Reba. So many things are different with Gypsy Rose." She wiped her eyes. "It's so **frustrating**."

"Hannah!" barked Miss Jill from her horse, Ziggy. She was waiting at the top of the track. "Didn't I say stay where

I could see you? Didn't I say *don't* go down this track?"

"Miss Jill, please don't be mad with Hannah," **pleaded** Bella. "I took Gypsy Rose to the creek and … well …"

"Go on," said Miss Jill.

"Gypsy Rose wouldn't cross the creek until Hannah and Jin Jin showed up."

"Jin Jin must have heard Gypsy Rose when we were in the top paddock," explained Hannah. "He just **took off**. I know you said don't go down the track, but I couldn't stop him."

"I'm lucky they came," said Bella. "Turns out Gypsy Rose trusts Jin Jin more than she trusts me." She looked down and **picked** at the edge of her saddle.

"The more time you spend with Gypsy Rose, the more she'll trust you," said Miss Jill. She was less upset now she knew both girls were safe. "You have to put time in with a new pony, Bella. Get to know the pony you have, not the pony you have in your head. In time she'll like the creek just as much as Reba does."

Miss Jill turned to Jin Jin and Hannah. The pony's ears **flicked** back and forth and he looked away.

"Jin Jin can be **quite a rocket** when he wants to be," Miss Jill said and smiled. "Just make sure he doesn't start thinking he's the boss, Hannah." She turned Ziggy around. "You did well to help your friend. Put Jin Jin in Gypsy Rose's paddock this afternoon. She clearly likes his company."

43

As Miss Jill headed for the jumping arena, Bella and Hannah walked their ponies towards the paddocks.

"You can tell Jin Jin **really trusts** you," said Bella. "You're going to be a good team."

"You and Gypsy Rose will be a great team too," said Hannah.

"I hope so," sighed Bella. "Riding is never as special when you're not. Sorry for getting you into trouble, Hannah. I'll see you down at the paddock." Bella rode ahead.

Hannah thought about what Miss Jill had said: "Get to know the pony you have, not the pony you have in your head."

Hannah looked down at her pony's **scruffy** neck and rubbed it. Jin Jin looked nothing like her wish pony. He was a big-headed, short-legged skewbald but he felt so much like hers. Jin Jin didn't look like it on the outside, but he really was the clever, kind and trusting pony she'd wished for.

PONY PROFILE

Name: Jin Jin

Rider: Hannah

Owner: Saddleback Stables

Age: 10

Breed: Australian Stock Horse cross Shetland pony

Height: 13 hands

Temperament: mischievous, confident, independent, reliable

Coat: skewbald (white patches on a chestnut coat)

Markings: tobiano (a special kind of skewbald, with rounded, white patches on the body, and chestnut on the head and chest)

Habits: sniffs and nudges for carrots, apples and other treats. Tosses his head when he doesn't want to do something. Flicks his ears when paying attention.

Likes: treats, being brushed, scratches between his ears

Dislikes: competitions, especially games, and getting on a horse float

Did you know? There are many types of painted horses. Skewbald means any colour other than black with white patches. Piebald means black and white, like a magpie. These beautiful markings are also called "paint".

GLOSSARY

 bridle
a harness around a pony's head to guide it

 canter
a pony's pace, between a trot and a gallop, with at least one foot on the ground at any time

 jodhpurs
full-length riding pants

 mesmerised
fascinated

 stirrups
rings hanging below the saddle to support the rider's feet

 **tack**
riding equipment, such as saddles and bridles